Bear & Katie

in

The Riverboat Ride

(on the Ohio)

By Loni R. Burchett

Illustrated by Patricia Sweet-MacDonald

Written by Loni R. Burchett
Illustrated by Patricia Sweet-MacDonald
Edited by Nancy Grossman and Joanie Bennett

Published by
Black Lab Publishing, LLC
P.O. Box 64
Alton, NH 03809
blacklabpub@hotmail.com
www.bearandkatie.com

Printed by Morgan Press, Manchester, NH
603-624-6880
Published and manufactured in the U.S.A.

First Printing: April, 2006

ISBN: 0-9742815-3-0

Dedicated to

Robert Anders, my uncle, whose intelligence and love for history was a great influence in my life.

The people who worked and traveled by riverboat, and for their hard work building our towns and cities.

And to Bear and Katie forever: who truly lived up to the old saying; "A dog is a man's best friend."

Special Thanks:

Nancy Grossman
Artist, writer, editor and wonderful friend

Jill Skaggs
Woolard Elementary
Manchester, Ohio

Eunice Duley (Aunt Noonie)

Lucette Brehm
For providing information about the *Delta Queen*

David Karem and Linda Harris
For their help and information about the *Belle of Louisville*

Acknowledgements:

Belle of Louisville Waterfront Development Corp.
129 East River Road
Louisville, Kentucky 40202

The Delta Queen Steamboat Company
Robin Street Wharf
1380 Port of New Orleans Place
New Orleans, Louisiana 70130

Boyd County Public Library
Ashland, Kentucky
Judy Fleming
Jim Kettel
Jim Powers

Preface

Over 100 years ago, during the late 1800s and early 1900s, huge riverboats, also known as steamboats and paddlewheels, dominated the Ohio, Mississippi, Missouri and other large rivers. Not only were they well known for their beauty, but they were an important part of our industry. Riverboats were used to haul cattle, building materials, and eventually were used to push barges filled with oil and coal up and down the waterways.

But it was the excitement of traveling on a riverboat that became America's favorite pastime. That tradition lives on today. From tours on the Hudson River in New York to the Columbia River in Oregon, people are fascinated by the beauty and history of these magnificent boats.

NOTE: Bear wears a red collar. Katie prefers to wear a blue scarf.

Bear and Katie always refer to their owners as Dad and Mom.

Table of Contents

Introduction:

Folks in the South say there's nothing more exciting and more fun than a ride on a riverboat. These gigantic boats that travel our southern waterways that cut through the heartland of America have become the luxury liners of the rivers.

Some might say they are like "river hotels". Decorated with elegance, the dining rooms and ballrooms are a fascinating sight. The Victorian look of yesterday captivates everyone who takes a tour on one of these beautiful riverboats.

The heart of these giant boats is the steam engines, consisting of tubes, cylinders, gauges and valves, which propel the huge paddlewheel at the back of the boat. The paddlewheel is considered one of the most beautiful features of the riverboat.

Bear and Katie are unaware that they are about to journey into the world of riverboats. When they stumble upon an authentic steam-powered paddlewheel, with its tall stacks and the beautiful sound of the calliope playing, how can they resist? So...come along and take a riverboat ride with Bear and Katie.

The Riverboat Ride

(on the Ohio)

It's a beautiful day and the Memorial Day weekend is quickly approaching. Every year the family takes a trip out of town, just like millions of other families across America.

This year Mom and Dad and Bear and Katie will be attending a family reunion in Kentucky. Mom and Dad have a lot of relatives there, and it's where Bear and Katie were born. This will be an exciting trip for the two Black Labs.

Dad and Mom are packing the truck for the long trip. Bear and Katie are helping too. They are gathering the things they want to take.

"Katie, don't forget your favorite rug you like to sleep on," barks Bear.

"And don't forget that fluffy cushion you spend hours sleeping on every day, you lazy dog," chuckles Katie.

Bear just lets out a soft growl. The two are so happy to be taking a trip to visit family so far away.

"Don't forget your leashes, girls!" yells Mom from another room. Bear and Katie both bark to let her know they have their leashes. They pick them up with their teeth and take them outside to Dad, with Mom at their heels.

"Good girls!" he tells them with a pat on each dog's head. "Well then...I believe we have everything."

"Oops! I forgot the camera," cries Mom. "I'll be right back."

Meanwhile, Dad helps Bear and Katie into the truck. The two settle in and make themselves comfortable.

Mom returns with the camera, then stops to take a picture of Bear and Katie setting in the back seats. "Well...now we can go," she says.

It's a long trip from New Hampshire to Kentucky. Bear and Katie want to see how far it is. Mom gets out a map, but Bear and Katie don't understand it at all. So Mom takes a piece of paper and draws a few simple lines for them to read. Bear and Katie don't understand that any better than the map, but decide to oblige Mom by pretending they understand.

"We better get some rest." ruffs Katie. Mom smiles, reaches out her hand and rubs each of them behind an ear. "You know, girls, you just might see a riverboat while we are there. The reunion party is right on the Ohio River. There are barges and riverboats that travel it daily," she tells them with a smile.

Bear and Katie enjoy listening to Mom talk about her home town, but quickly turn their attention to something else.

"What I like about this trip," says Katie, "is all the food we will get to eat when we get there. I can see beans, 'taters and cornbread swirling in my head."

"Oh, yes!" barks Bear, picturing all the food. "I can't wait for the biscuits and gravy, and you mustn't forget the fried green tomatoes! Yum...yum!" she shakes her head in gleeful anticipation.

"Yuck! Yuck!" barks Katie. "Fried green tomatoes! You're ruining my appetite!" she cries.

Bear just shrugs off Katie's remarks. "All this talk about food is making me hungry, tired and sleepy," gripes Bear. "I think I will take a nice long nap. Just wake me up when you see the sign that says, 'Welcome to Kentucky, the Blue Grass State.'"

"Ok," replies Katie with a big yawn. "It's a long trip and I guess we may as well take advantage of it and get ourselves a nice, long nap." Katie's eyes close slightly as she continues to think. "I wonder why they call it bluegrass? It sure looked like the grass was green the last time I saw it," Katie mumbles, as the hum of the tires lulls her off to sleep.

Hundreds of miles and many long hours later, they arrive in Kentucky. Aunts, uncles, cousins and lots of family dogs are there to greet them. Bear and Katie are eager to go for a walk, stretch their legs and get a drink of water.

Dad whistles to Bear and Katie. "don't go far, girls," he shouts. Bear and Katie both bark to let him know they've heard him. Then they walk slowly toward the woods, working out miles and miles of stiffness as they go.

"You know, Bear, we are really going to see a lot of squirrels here," says Katie, peering up at a tall pine tree.

Bear looks up at the tree and begins to wag her tail. "And I have a feeling Uncle Tommy is going to want to take us on a coon hunt," Bear smiles.

"You mean chase raccoons?" cries Katie.

"That's what I mean, chase raccoons," replies Bear.

Still gazing up at the tall pine tree, she

remembers Chief and Jane when they were just puppies. "Katie, we're no match for those two hound dogs," she continues.

"I suppose, we better head back to the house and help unload the truck," says Katie with a sigh. "I really enjoy walking through the woods and reminiscing." She smiles.

"We'll be doing plenty of that tomorrow at the reunion," Bear reminds her.

Bear and Katie return to find the truck empty. Everyone is on the porch, laughing and catching up on old times.

Katie takes a place on the porch near Dad, and Bear lies down near Mom. "Tomorrow is going to be a lot of fun for you and Bear," Dad tells Katie. "The two of you are going to meet a lot of kin folk, and Uncle Tommy will be eager

to take you on a hunt with Chief and Jane.
Aunt Noonie will be having the pleasure of
cooking the meal."

"Oh, boy!" barks Bear. "The best cook in the
entire state of Kentucky is going to cook at the
reunion."

Katie closes her eyes for a moment and
thinks about the food. "I can't wait," she cries.
"It makes my mouth water. I can taste the food
already. Mmm mmm!"

"Well then, let's get you two to bed, because
tomorrow will be a big day for you," says Dad,
rising to his feet. Bear and Katie jump to their
feet and run inside the house. Everyone laughs
as they watch the two labs search for a
comfortable place to sleep.

Bear and Katie are so excited about going to

the reunion, they quickly fall off to sleep. Mom and Dad tiptoe past their two lovable labs to their bed. They know tomorrow will be a good day for Bear and Katie to meet everyone.

But as Dad brushes his teeth, he finds himself worrying about what Katie might do. She has a habit of running off on her own, especially when she sees water, and the reunion is at the park down by the river.

Still mumbling about Katie, Dad slips into bed and turns off the light.

"Oh well...I'll just have to keep a close eye on her," he thinks to himself as he falls off to sleep.

The next morning Katie wakes first. Jumping to her feet, she shakes herself off, then she calls to Bear. "Bear, let's go for a walk before everyone wakes up," she barks. Bear's eyes pop open. She rubs them with her paws and shakes herself awake. Like Katie, she is excited about getting an early breakfast and a walk before they leave to go to the reunion.

"We need to eat light, because there's going to be a lot of Aunt Noonie's food to eat today. We don't want to stuff ourselves too soon," Bear snickers.

When they return, they are surprised to see everyone is up and ready to go. Dad grabs a few lawn chairs to take along. Then he helps his two labs into the truck.

It's not far to the park where the reunion is being held. They notice a large crowd gathering down near the edge of the river. "Wow!" ruffs Katie, looking at all the people. "Do you think all of them are Dad and Mom's family?" she asks as Dad parks the truck.

"I'm sure they are," answers Bear. "This is just too cool! We are going to have so much fun!"

"Oh, look! People are playing Frisbee! I'm sure they need me!" yelps Katie, as she jumps from the truck and immediately takes off, running in the direction of the Frisbee swirling in the air just above her head.

Bear, looking at Dad shakes her head. "That's Katie for you. She'll never change," she says with a chuckle. Dad rubs Bear on the head.

The park is filling up with people fast. Bear and Katie are having fun playing Frisbee and retrieving balls.

A small group of children approaches Bear

and Katie. "My name is Josh," says one of the boys. "This is my sister Allison, and these are some of my cousins. Kenneth is from California. Jerry came all the way from Washington State, and Taylor – she lives across the river in Ohio. Dirk, he's a Kentucky boy like me. We hear you are Bear and Katie, our Uncle Charlie and Aunt Doris's famous Black Labs. We're happy you two came all the way from New England to meet us," he says with a smile.

"So...how about we play some ball?" Josh continues. "I'll pitch...Dirk can bat first. Jerry can catch. Kenneth, Taylor and Allison, you three play the bases, and Bear and Katie can play the outfield. If the ball goes down towards the river, Bear and Katie can retrieve it for us." They all cheer and Bear and Katie, of course, are happy to help out.

They all begin to play ball. Bear and Katie can smell the aroma of Aunt Noonie's cooking and can't wait for the feast. Dirk hits the ball too far and it lands down at the edge of the river. Katie runs to retrieve it. With the ball in her mouth, she turns to return to the game, when suddenly she spots something she has never seen before.

Katie drops the ball and barks for Bear to join her. Bear runs to Katie to see what has taken her mind off the ball game.

Josh sees Katie drop the ball and watches Bear run to meet Katie. He decides the two labs don't want to play ball anymore, so he picks up another ball and the children continue their game.

Bear reaches Katie at the river. "What do you want, Katie?"

"Look...at...that, Bear! What is that?" barks Katie, excited.

"Why, I believe it's what Mom and Dad were talking about. I think it's a riverboat," answers Bear. "That is the most beautiful boat I ever saw in my life."

"Look at the size of it!" shouts Katie. "It must be four decks high."

"It's a gigantic riverboat. It's called the *Belle of Louisville*. It's not only the most beautiful boat I ever saw, it's the biggest boat I ever saw. It's beautiful, just beautiful," whispers Bear.

Katie's eyes are fixed on the vessel tied up to the dock. "Let's take a closer look," she whines.

Bear knows Katie is curious and she's a bit curious, too. "Ok...Katie but we have to hurry before anyone notices we are missing," she ruffs.

As they get closer, they see passengers boarding the giant paddlewheel for a trip down the Ohio River. Great puffs of lavender smoke belching from its smokestacks trail off into the blue morning sky.

"I wonder if we can sneak on board and take a look?" says Katie.

"I don't know. I think we would be wise to go back to playing ball," groans Bear. "Looking is one thing. Going on board is a whole different matter."

Bear is beginning to worry about Katie's fascination with the beautiful giant riverboat.

"I really think we need to be getting back to the party," she says, already wishing she had never said a word to encourage Katie.

"But I just want to see what it looks like inside," Katie whines. "Then we can go back to the party and no one will even know we were gone."

"Ok, Katie, but we really must make it a quick tour," cries Bear, with a worried look on her face.

Bear pulls up close to Katie. The two of them linger while all the passengers board the big paddlewheel, waiting for the perfect time to sneak on board. They look both ways. Nobody's looking. Bear and Katie quickly sneak up the plank and onto the beautiful riverboat.

Bear spots an open door. "Katie," she says with a soft woof. "Let's go over to that open door and take a look."

The two of them quietly crawl to the open door.

The first thing Katie sees is an enormous table draped with beautifully decorated tablecloths, piled high with a huge buffet, enough food to feed a shipload of hungry passengers. The smell of food fills the air.

"I'm going over there!" she whispers to Bear.

"I don't think that's a good idea, Katie. We'll get caught for sure," grumbles Bear.

"We can hide under the table. No one will see us," wheedles Katie.

Bear has a feeling that Katie is just after the

food. Bear's a bit hungry, but she wants to wait and eat what Aunt Noonie is fixing at the reunion.

"If we can get to the tables, we can sneak through the door behind them, take a quick tour and get off the boat," Katie assures Bear, knowing that's what Bear wants to hear.

The two labs wait for a quiet moment, then look both ways. They don't see anyone.

"All right...let's go!" whispers Bear. They race across the room and quickly duck under the table.

"There, you see? I told you this would be a good place to hide," whispers Katie. Then Katie decides to help herself to some food.

"I knew it!" says Bear. "You were after the food all the time."

"No, I wasn't Bear, but since it's here, we
may as well help ourselves to some," whispers
Katie as she reaches for a drumstick. "What do
you want, Bear?"

"I really shouldn't be doing this, but I'll take
a piece of ham," barks Bear quietly. But just as

Katie reaches for the ham, her paw gets caught
on the tablecloth and the ham – and everything
else – crashes to the floor.

Everyone looks to see what the racket is all about and Bear and Katie are spotted. A man in a uniform reaches under the table and grabs Katie by her scarf. Bear jumps out from under the table and startles the man enough that he loses his grip on Katie.

"Let's go, Katie!" shouts Bear, heading back for the gangplank. But when they get there, they discover it has been raised. The huge paddlewheel is slowly picking up speed. They have already pulled away from the shore!

Bear and Katie are heading down river and far away from their loved ones.

The man in the uniform catches up with the two Black Labs. Bear and Katie notice the man quickly approaching and the two of them take off running.

The man sees some passengers standing farther down by the railing looking at the passing scenery. "Stop those dogs! Stop those dogs!" he shouts to them. "They're not supposed to be on this boat."

One of the men at the railing charges after Bear and Katie. Bear's quick thinking comes in handy. "This way, Katie. Follow me," Bear woofs as she ducks through an open door with Katie at her heels.

The door slams shut and the two labs heave a sigh. "We've outsmarted that man," says Katie.

Wrong. The man shows up again, but just in time, Bear spots a stairway.

Bear thinks quickly. "Up or down? We can run down faster," she decides and down the two race. By the time the man gets to the stairway, there's no clue which way the Black Labs might have gone. Bear and Katie have gotten away.

The captain calls down from the upper deck, "Someone find those stowaway dogs!"

"Oh, no!" woofs Katie. "I hope they don't throw me overboard! I'm a good swimmer but I don't know in which direction to swim. What will I do?"

Bear nudges Katie. "What will you do! What about me? I don't even swim. Your curiosity has gotten us into some serious trouble this time! No question. We need to stick together if we are going to get back to shore," she grumbles.

"I'm sorry, Bear. I feel awful." Cries Katie, her head hanging down.

Bear looks at her best friend. She knows Katie feels terribly about getting them into trouble, and she knows Katie didn't mean to cause any harm. It's just a case of Katie being Katie. "Oh, forget it," replies Bear, kindly. "It's my fault too. I wanted to see this beautiful boat as much as you did."

"You really mean that, Bear?" asks Katie gratefully, smiling at Bear.

"Yeah, yeah!" answers Bear with a bit of a snarl.

As soon as the coast is clear, Bear and Katie sneak over to the railing and look to see where they are. There's no sign of the shore where the family reunion is taking place. Katie looks over her shoulder at Bear, a worried expression on her face. "I don't know where we are going and where the boat will stop," she moans. "I'm really scared."

"Me, too," cries Bear with sigh. "But we mustn't let our fears get the best of us."

Suddenly, out of nowhere, a young boy appears. "Hi there, pooches!" says the young boy. "Where did you come from? Are you lost? can't you find you family?" Too many questions at once make Bear and Katie nervous.

Katie sits down and wags her tail. Bear stares, at attention. The two of them look at the boy with their sad brown eyes.

"Well!" exclaims Katie. "You see we snuck on this big boat to tour it."

"We had no idea that it would leave the dock with us on it," continues Bear.

"Oh, no! You poor, poor dogs!" Says the boy stroking them on the head.

"How will anyone ever find us?" Katie asks their new friend, hanging her head. "They don't know we are on the boat."

"I miss the family already," cries Bear. She slowly lies down and tucks her paws under her chin and begins to whine.

"You'll be okay," says the young boy. "My name is Matthew. My grandfather and I make this trip every year. It brings back old memories for Gramps. He was just a kid like me when he used to ride one of these big old paddlewheels with his daddy," he continues.

"We are Bear and Katie. We are visiting family for the holiday and we're suppose to be playing ball at a family reunion, somewhere back that way in Kentucky," sighs Bear.

"Can you tell us where we are going?" asks Katie.

"I'm not sure, but my Gramps will know. And he'll know where we can hide you two, so you won't get caught," Matthew assures them. "So follow me, before that mean captain comes back and chases you again."

Bear and Katie happily follow their new friend Matthew.

Back at the reunion, everyone is busy playing games and reminiscing. Suddenly, Dad realizes he hasn't seen Bear and Katie for a while.

Surely Bear would be hanging around where Aunt Noonie is preparing the food. She'd be making sure Noonie needed her assistance, especially as a taster, he thinks to himself. And, of course, Katie would want to go for a swim, seeing they are so close to the water.

Something doesn't seem right and Dad begins to worry.

Looking around, Dad notices that Josh and the others are still playing ball, but Bear and Katie are no where in sight. He quickly approaches Josh and the others. "Weren't Bear and Katie playing ball with you earlier?" he asks them.

"They were indeed," replies Kenneth. "Dirk was up to bat and he hit the ball way down by the river. Katie ran after it and Bear followed her, but they never came back. So we got another ball and continued on with our game."

Suddenly, Taylor pushes her way to the
front of the little crowd and peeks her head in
between Allison and Jerry. "Uncle Charlie...I
saw Katie and Bear wandering down by the

boat dock. A huge riverboat was parked there and I saw Bear and Katie standing over where the passengers were boarding. Do you think they might have gotten on the boat?" she cries.

"Oh, my! I sure hope they didn't," says Dad with a groan.

Dad nervously rubs his head with his hat, as to adjust it as he wipes the sweat from his forehead with his other hand. He knows how curious Katie can be, and if she saw the boat, she most likely got on it to take a look. Knowing Bear, she would probably follow Katie to keep her out of trouble.

"I better go over to the dock and ask if anyone may have seen Bear and Katie. I also need to find out where that riverboat is going," Dad tells them.

Dad quickly gives Mom the bad news and suggests she stay with the family while he goes to look for Bear and Katie. "I'm sure they will be hungry when I find them. You be sure Aunt Noonie saves some chicken and dumplings for them," he calls back over his shoulder as he rushes to his truck.

Just as he's climbing into the truck, Josh and the others show up. "we're going with you, Uncle Charlie," says Josh. "We can help find them. Our parents already know we're going with you."

"Taylor and Kenneth, the two of you stay behind with Mom," shouts Dad, with a wave of his hand. "Just in case Bear and Katie are not on the boat, the two of you can keep them entertained while we are gone. The rest of you come with me."

Josh and Dirk jump in the front seat with Dad, while Allison and Jerry get in the back seat. And off they go to find Bear and Katie.

Searching for Two Black Labs

Dad arrives at the boat dock, he jumps out of the truck and quickly goes to the ticket office which is closed by now. He looks around and spots a man standing by an old flatboat that's been converted into a beautiful houseboat.

"Excuse me, sir! I'm looking for two Black Labs. They wandered off from back over there," he says, pointing to where the reunion is taking place.

"Why, yes!...did one have on a blue scarf and both dogs a little on the hefty side?" asks the man.

"Oh, yes! That would be my Bear and Katie," replies Dad.

"I saw them wander onto that big old paddlewheel that was docked here a while ago.

I can't say as I saw them get off," says the man.

"Do you have any idea where It's headed?" asks Dad, nervously.

"I'm not sure. Maybe Cincinnati, or even St. Louis. I really don't know," comes the answer.

Dad is getting very worried and begins to think the worst. "Would Katie jump and try to swim? Would Bear try to follow her? That would be awful. Bear doesn't swim and Katie wouldn't know which way to go". Says Dad, mumbling out loud.

"Don't worry, Uncle Charlie," says Josh in a quiet voice. "Bear is so smart, she would never let Katie swim. And Katie would never leave Bear on the boat by herself."

"Of course! You're right. I should know better. What am I thinking?" Dad exclaims. "Those two dogs are always there for each other, and with Bear's quick thinking, they will find some way to let me know they are in trouble," he continues.

Just as Dad returns to the truck, he spots a man coming out of the ticket office. He rushes to talk to him.

"Sir, the riverboat that just left, where is it going? I believe my dogs are on the boat."

"The *Belle of Louisville*? Why, It's bound for Cincinnati, then on to Louisville, and then finally to St. Louis," answers the man.

Dad turns with a sad look on his face and begins to walk away. He is worried he may never find his beautiful dogs.

"But the boat does stop in a small town down river called Maysville," the man calls after him. "If you leave now, you might beat the boat there. Depends on the traffic, you know."

Dad dashes to the truck. He tells the children they are going to go to Maysville to meet the riverboat. The children cheer!

"I know a back road!" shouts Josh. "Uncle Tommy comes this way to go coon hunting, and I know the roads by heart."

Dad is glad he brought the children with him. They are proving to be very helpful and good company.

Back at the boat, Bear and Katie follow Matthew to a small cabin on an upper deck. "Gramps always rents this cabin because it's one of the original rooms that some of the most famous riverboat gamblers used to stay in. He'll tell you all about them," Matthew says as he opens the door.

"Matthew! Where have you been?" grumbles a little old man with white hair, sitting by a window peering out at the beautiful Kentucky landscape.

"Well...I...found two new friends, Gramps," says Matthew. With his arm around both dogs, he moves closer to the old man. "Gramps, this is Bear," he tells his grandfather, rubbing her on the head. "And this is Katie. They are lost and...I'm helping them."

"You don't say," says Gramps. "Two Black Labs! Well, now I've seen everything. Come closer now. I'm Matthew's grandpa," he tells Bear and Katie, waving his hand at them with a big smile on his face. "Tell me, how did you two critters end up on this big old paddle-wheel?"

"Well, we were at a family reunion and we saw this beautiful riverboat, and we thought we'd take a quick tour, but Katie spotted food...and...well...." Bear stops short to take a look at Katie, and then continues, "Anyway, the boat took off with us still on board."

"That mean old captain began to chase us, but Matthew came to our rescue," whines Katie. "we're lost. We just have to find our way back to the reunion."

"Don't you girls worry. I know every inch of these rivers. Matthew and I will make sure you get back to that reunion safe," Gramps assures them.

Bear and Katie begin to relax. Bear lies down by Gramps' feet and Katie takes a place next to Matthew.

"Tell us about this beautiful, huge boat," suggests Bear with a soft bark.

Gramps leans back in his chair and reaches for a deck of cards that could easily be as old as he is. Shuffling them, he takes a long look out the window.

"These riverboats were known as paddlewheels, back in the old days. Some folks called them steamboats. They burned wood to heat water in their boilers, which generated steam to run their engines. You could see the smoke from their huge stacks from miles away. You could hear them coming, too, and hear the music playing," he tells them with a pleasant smile.

"At one time, steamboats were the best way to travel. People went in search of their dreams. Small settlements began to grow in America's heartland. Those settlements grew into towns, and the towns grew into cities, stretching all up and down the Mississippi, the Missouri and the Ohio Rivers. These beautiful boats took passengers from Pittsburgh to St. Louis and from Minneapolis all the way down to New Orleans," he continues.

"Oh yes...some towns grew big and some stayed small. Pittsburg became an industrial town, along with Wheeling, Huntington, Cincinnati, Louisville, Owensboro, Evansville, St Louis, St. Paul and New Orleans. The towns stretch all the way to the mouth of the Mississippi River. Oh, but we can't forget the smaller towns like Ashland, Kentucky. That's where you girls got on this beautiful boat," he tells them as he pauses to take a look at Bear and Katie, sitting stock-still, listening to every word.

"And let's see...well, there's Manchester, one of the first settlements in the whole state of Ohio. There's Ironton, Portsmouth, historical Greenup and of course Maysville, Kentucky. That's where we are headed now. On down river there's Augusta, Newport and...oh my!" Gramps pauses for a moment, then continues.

"Let me tell you a little about St. Louis, Missouri. I call it 'St. Louie.' That town was what they called "The gateway to the West!" Not only did hundreds of riverboats travel there, but it was the gathering place for covered wagons. You see...after arriving in St. Louis by boat, people traveled across land in covered wagons to build new settlements on the prairies. That riverboat town is something to see!"

Gramps stops and looks down at the two dogs. "You do know where the names of the rivers come from, right?" Bear and Katie both look abashed. Gramps chuckles. "I reckoned you might not. Might as well clear that up right now."

Gramps scratches his chin a moment. "Let's see if I can get this right. The Missouri was named for a particular tribe of Sioux Indians. It means the 'river of large canoes.' 'Ohio,' That's an Iroquois word. It means 'large' or 'beautiful river.' And the Mississippi — well that just depends who you ask. Some folks will tell you it means 'Father of Waters.' And some will say it means 'gathering of waters.' Whatever it means, it's a beautiful word, Mississippi. That one we got from the Chippewa."

Bear and Katie woof in agreement, then settle back down for more storytelling. They could tell that Gramps loved to tell his stories.

"Well, as I was saying, folks traveled the river to follow their dreams. Families rode these steamboats. So did outlaws and gamblers – all kinds of people." He pauses. "Let me tell you, these steamboats were luxurious, exciting and adventurous."

"Tell them the story about Pierre Marcel!" says Matthew eagerly.

Bear and Katie suspect Matthew has heard this story many times. It must be the one he enjoys the most of all the stories old Gramps tells.

"Yes, yes!" ruffs Katie. "We'd love to hear the story."

"Yes, please. We really want to know all about this Pierre Marcel," whines Bear, sitting up and moving in close to Gramps.

Gramps leans back in his chair, shuffles the deck of cards in his hand, takes a deep breath, then begins his story.

"It was at the turn of the century," he begins. "The twentieth century, that is, back in 1910. There was this Frenchman. They say he came down from Canada — Nova Scotia, I believe. They say he was the biggest gambler on the riverboats, ever. He traveled up and down the Mississippi. They called him Pierre Marcel, 'the Mississippi Man,'" Gramps tells them.

Bear and Katie are already intrigued. "This will be like a story right out of a Mark Twain novel," they thought. Knowing this will be an interesting story, they move in closer to Gramps. Katie rests her head on his feet, and

Bear rests her head on his lap. Matthew snuggles up close to Bear.

"Pierre was a man of about average height, I'd say...and had a husky build," Gramps begins. "Pierre had a home in the French Quarter of New Orleans. But they say he never lost his love for his beautiful Nova Scotia, up in Canada. He was a gambler, not much of a lady's man. But he had his eye on one special lady, if you know what I mean," says Gramps with a grin.

Bear and Katie look at Matthew with matching twinkles in their eyes.

"Go on, Gramps!" says Matthew, nudging him with one hand and stroking Bear on the head with his other.

"Her name was Margrette. Prettiest girl you ever laid your eyes on. She was tall and slim, with dark eyes and darker hair that hung to her waist. Pierre took one look at her and knew she was special, that she would change his life forever," the old man tells them.

"But it seems that gambling was Pierre's favorite pastime," continues Gramps. "He was known as the best poker player from Chicago to New Orleans. Pierre had accumulated a lot of money through the years, most of it won playing poker. He always said he was saving his money to build a farm some day. He had his eye on land he'd seen in Kansas, somewhere near Wichita, I believe it was," he says. Then his voice drops.

"One night during a poker game, a huge storm was brewing, with lightning and thunder like nothing you've ever seen. The big old riverboat began to rock back and forth. The winds became stronger and stronger. Everyone was frightened. Pierre became worried about the strength of the wind, wondering if the huge paddlewheel could hold up to it. Suddenly he thought of Margrette and rushed to check on her." The old man paused, then quickly went on. He was a great storyteller.

"Just as he entered the hallway to the rooms, the boat lurched. Pierre ran as quickly as he could to open Margrette's door, bouncing back and forth against the walls, trying to keep his balance. Reaching her door, he half pulled it off its hinges. And there he found Margrette, huddled in a corner, so frightened and so relieved to see that Pierre had come to her rescue." Katie gave a little bark of relief herself.

"Pierre took her by the hand and the two of them made their way up to the main deck. The large steamboat tipped back and forth, but stood its ground. After searching frantically, Pierre and Margrette found a safe place to wait out the storm until it passed — and that was right here, in this very room," Gramps ended with a dramatic flourish.

Bear and Katie bark with excitement at the thought that they are standing in the exact same room that had sheltered Pierre and Margrette from that terrible storm.

"I sure hope a storm like that doesn't happen while we are on board!" barks Katie.

"Me, too!" agrees Bear.

"Oh, don't worry about that!" shouts Matthew. "It's a beautiful day today. The sky is perfectly clear."

Gramps chuckles and then continues, "It was then that Pierre realized that his life of gambling and roaming the rivers was at an end. Margrette had changed everything," Gramps tells them, pausing for a moment. He shuffles his cards and looks around the room as if he is reliving the event, as if he actually knew these people.

"They say that Pierre left a fortune of money on the boat. It's been said that it was left in a burlap bag, hidden in one of the walls. But it was never found. I don't believe it to be true, because Pierre and Margrette moved to Kansas and went ahead and built that farm he'd always dreamed of. Personally, I think he took the money with him. I heard that he never returned to the river again," says Gramps.

"Now that's a story!" ruffs Katie with appreciation.

"You can say that again!" barks Bear, jumping to her feet and wagging her tail.

"I told you, Gramps can tell a good story!" boasts Matthew with a proud grin.

It's now 2:00 p.m. Dad and the kids are still driving along the river, hoping to spot the *Belle of Louisville*.

"The boat has been gone for a few hours," says Dirk, with an uncertain look.

Josh, Allison, and Jerry glance at Dirk and back to each other, reading the two questions on their faces that none of them wants to ask Dad: "Will we be able to find Bear and Katie? Are they lost forever?"

"It won't be long until we reach Maysville," Dad says. "I just hope the riverboat stops there."

"But doesn't the boat go to Louisville?" asks Allison.

"Yes, it does," replies Dad. "But the *Delta Queen* will be there today to pick up passengers for a trip to Pittsburg. So the *Belle of Louisville* might stop there, too, to exchange passengers."

"Oh my!" say Josh and Jerry at the same time. "What if Bear and Katie get on <u>that</u> boat?"

"Don't even think that," shouts Josh.

Dad interrupts the conversation. "Let's all try to think positive. We will find Bear and Katie soon!" he assures them.

Dirk motions for everyone to be silent. They know Dad is worried about Bear and Katie.

They turn their attention towards the river, all of them gazing out the window, each hoping to be the first to spot the huge boat.

Now that Gramps has told his story, Bear and Katie return to their worries about where they are going.

"Dad must know by now we are lost," cries Bear. "He never lets us go too far without checking on us."

"I wonder if Dad and Mom think we may have gotten on this boat," replies Katie. "If they do, then I know they will be coming after us."

"I'm getting hungry!" whines Bear, rubbing a paw on her stomach. "I'd sure like to be eating some of Aunt Noonie's chicken and dumplin's right now."

"Gee, I'd like to be eating a piece of Noonie's famous ham, smothered with glaze, nuts and raisins. Mmm, mmm!" replies Katie, slurping her tongue from one side of her mouth to the other.

"I sure do miss Dad and Mom," whimper Bear.

"Me, too," echoes Katie.

Bear and Katie lie down and tuck their paws under their chins. Matthew and Gramps look at each other sadly. Gramps knows Bear and Katie are scared and he knows that even though he has stories to tell them, the stories can't take away Bear and Katie's loneliness and yearnings for Dad and Mom.

Suddenly Gramps has an idea. He rushes out of the cabin and down to the galley, grabs a few chicken legs and heads up to the top deck to talk to the captain.

"Well...hello there, Gramps! As always, it's a pleasure to see you on one of our trips," the captain greets him as he turns to look out at the beautiful blue water flowing on the Ohio River.

"Well, you know how much I love the river," replies Gramps, returning the captain's smile. "I never get tired of riding these great old paddlewheels. I guess it's in my blood," he laughs. Gramps pauses, waiting for just the right moment to ask the captain about helping out Bear and Katie.

The captain takes off his hat, combs his fingers through his hair and puts his hat back on. He turns to Gramps with a puzzled look.

"By the way, you haven't seen two Black Labs hanging around the boat have you? I know how much you like animals," he says.

"Well, since you mentioned it, I was just going to talk to you about that," answers Gramps.

"I knew it!" shouts the captain. "I had a feeling someone was hiding them. You and Matthew, eh? I knew it!"

"Now take it easy, captain. They are sweet dogs," says Gramps.

"Sweet! Sweet, you say? Have you seen the dining room? They knocked over chairs and one of the dogs pulled on a tablecloth and brought all the food down. It's a mess in there!" shouts the captain.

"And that's why we need to help them get

back home," replies Gramps.

"I'd like to help them, all right, with a big old kick in their behinds," growls the captain.

"I know how you feel, really, but they are truly sweet dogs, once you get to know them," says Gramps, patting the captain on the back to assure him. "Bear and Katie are fine dogs. I know where they are, and they're really scared. We need to find a way to get them back to where they got on the boat. I believe it was up around Ashland," he finishes.

The captain takes off his hat again, runs his fingers through his hair again, shuffles his feet, takes a deep breath and grumbles quietly. "All right, all right!" he says. "We are on our way to Cincinnati, and then to Louisville. But...we're almost to Maysville where the *Delta Queen* will be docked. I suppose I can persuade the

captain of the *Delta Queen* into taking the dogs back to Ashland. They are scheduled to stop in Ashland anyway. Let me see what I can do," says the captain gruffly. "But they better behave themselves, because the captain of the *Delta Queen* won't put up with them stealing food from the dinning room," he continues with a stern look.

Gramps quickly hides the two chicken legs he grabbed for Bear and Katie behind his back.

"I can promise you they'll be on their best behavior!" Gramps assures the captain. "Thank you. Thank you so much, Captain. Bear and Katie sure will be glad to hear that they are going back to the reunion."

Gramps heads back to give the good news to Bear and Katie, who are still lying on the floor with their paws tucked under their chins.

Bear and Katie look at each other and whine. "Gramps, I feel so sorry for them," says Matthew with a sigh.

"Well, feel sorry no more!" shouts Gramps. "Bear and Katie, you're going back home!"

Bear jumps to her feet, and Katie quickly follows. "We are? Oh boy! Oh boy!" ruff the two Black Labs, jumping on Gramps and almost knocking him to the ground.

"The captain said he is going to stop at Maysville and get the two of you a ride back on the *Delta Queen*, which is headed back to Ashland, where you got on the boat in the first place," he tells them.

Bear and Katie run out of Gramps' cabin and up to the observation deck. They jump up, placing their paws on the railing of the boat.

Gramps and Matthew run to catch up with Bear and Katie. Matthew points to the town of Maysville in the distance. They can also see the beautiful *Delta Queen*, already docked there.

Bear and Katie are so excited they set to howling. They howl and howl. Everyone on the boat comes to see what all the excitement is about. They all begin to laugh and cheer for the two pretty black dogs.

Gramps takes the two chicken legs out of his pocket and gives one each to Bear and Katie. Bear and Katie enjoy the chicken as the *Belle of Louisville* edges its way towards the dock where they will change riverboats and finally get back to the reunion party.

"You must go with us," ruffs Katie. "Everyone will be so happy to meet you."

"Oh, yes!" barks Bear. "You can enjoy Aunt Noonie's good cooking. Chicken and dumplin's! Yummm, yummm."

Gramps thinks about it for a moment.

"I would really like to join you and meet your fine family and, of course, try some of Aunt Noonie's chicken and dumplin's, but Matthew and I really have to be in St. Louis by tomorrow. But I promise you that next year we will be sure to be at the family reunion," Gramps promises his two new friends.

"Oh yes," shouts Matthew, "and I will make sure Gramps has plenty more riverboat stories to tell."

Bear and Katie marvel at the beautiful *Delta Queen* as the *Belle of Louisville* pulls to the dock right beside it. They are excited, not only to see another riverboat, but to get to travel on it as well. But they are especially excited to be going back to the reunion.

They say their good-byes to Gramps and Matthew.

"Thank you so much for everything," barks Bear politely.

"Thanks for hiding us, and for telling us a great story," ruffs Katie, sad to leave her new friends.

"We will miss the two of you," says Gramps.

Matthew wipes a tear from his eye and waves to Bear and Katie. "I'll never forget you, Bear and Katie," he shouts.

As the two Black Labs head up the gangplank to board the *Delta Queen*, its giant

calliope is playing so loud they can hardly hear
Gramps and Matthew saying good-bye to them.

Bear and Katie turn back, wave their paws
and howl to Gramps and Matthew until they
are out of sight.

Gramps and Matthew turn to walk back to the *Belle of Louisville* when a truck suddenly pulls up near the dock. Out jumps a man and four kids, all running towards the *Belle of Louisville*. Gramps and Matthew can see that the man is excited about something. Matthew hears one of the boys say, "I just hope Bear and Katie are here!"

Gramps hurries over to the man. "Sir? Did I hear you say you're looking for a Bear and a Katie?"

"Why, yes!" says Dad anxiously. "They're my dogs. I believe they may have gotten aboard this riverboat."

"Do you know them? Do you know where they are?" asks Dirk, excitedly.

"Have you seen them?" shouts Jerry,

standing right behind Dirk. Dad motions for the kids to calm down. He knows they are as anxious as he is to find Bear and Katie.

"Actually, yes, I have seen them. In fact my grandson, Matthew, and I took care of them on the boat," he answers with a big grin. "They sure are fine dogs, that Bear and Katie. Of course, you already know that. Matthew and I truly enjoyed ourselves with them," he continues. "Excuse my manners. I'm known around here as Gramps," he says, extending a hand to Dad.

"Pleased to meet you, Gramps," says a relieved Dad, shaking Gramps' hand warmly. "Pleased to meet you indeed. I'm Charlie."

"And I bet you want to know where they are right now," says Matthew, looking at the kids. Before they can answer him, he points up river to the riverboat that is now pulling *almost* out of sight.

Dad just sighs. "Oh, no! Now what will we do?" he wonders out loud, shaking his head.

"Don't worry, my friend. They are on their way back to the reunion party," laughs Gramps. "I asked the captain of the *Delta Queen* to take them home."

Dad lets out a long sigh of relief. "Well, then...I guess we will just have to get back in the truck and go back to the reunion."

Dad and the kids turn and head back to the truck. Dad suddenly stops and turns around to look back at Gramps and Matthew.

"Gramps!" he shouts. "How about you and Matthew come with us?"

"We'd love to, Charlie, but we have to be in St Louis tomorrow," answers Gramps.

"It sure would be nice to have you with us. It would sure make Bear and Katie two happy Black Labs."

"Yes!" shout the kids, excited. "Bear and Katie would be so surprised. They'd love to introduce you to the family."

Gramps pauses for a moment and looks at Matthew. "Well, I guess we could make St. Louis day after tomorrow. What do you think?"

Matthew jumps up and shouts, "Yes! Yes! This is just too...cool!"

Matthew introduces himself to the kids and they all climb in the back seat of the truck. Dad and Gramps enjoy each other's company all the way back to the reunion.

Bear and Katie pick seats on the top deck of the *Delta Queen*. This time they don't have to hide. The two of them get plenty of attention.

"This is really nice," ruffs Katie. "I love having the sun beam down on my face. It feels so relaxing!"

"And I enjoy the smell of fresh air, and the warm breeze, too," replies Bear.

"I really enjoy looking at the trees along the river bank. Kentucky on one side of the river and Ohio on the other," mumbles Bear.

"It's especially pretty seeing it from this magnificent riverboat. I love riverboats!" says Katie with a huge smile.

"Gramps said there's one called the *American Queen* and it has maybe six decks," yelps Bear.

"Six decks! Wow! Maybe the next time we can see that one," ruffs Katie all excited.

Bear jumps to her feet. "What do you *mean* next time?"

Katie thinks quickly. "I...mean, when they have Derby Day we can ask for another ride,"

"Oh, yes!" cries Bear. "You mean, Kentucky Derby Week. The town of Louisville has their annual Riverboat Races. *The American Queen, Delta Queen, Mississippi Queen, The Spirit of Jefferson* and *The Belle of Louisville* are all there to race on this very long river."

"We must talk to Dad about it. After all, he

mentioned taking us to see a horse race,"
agrees Bear. "And all this talk is making me a
bit hungry again. I'll be glad to see what Aunt
Noonie cooked at the reunion."

"Me, too! Until then, do you think they'd
care if we help ourselves to a snack in the
dining room?" snickers Katie.

"I wouldn't push it, Katie. They just might
help you off the boat," ruffs Bear.

"You mean - throw me overboard?" whines
Katie in alarm.

"That's exactly what I mean," chuckles Bear.

"Well then, I'll just finish this old chicken
leg Gramps gave me," barks Katie.

Bear and Katie are finally having a good

time, without a worry in the world. Soon they will be back at the reunion and with Dad, Mom and all the relatives. For the rest of this trip, they can enjoy themselves.

Mom and Aunt Noonie spot a riverboat approaching.

"Look, Noonie, there's another riverboat," Mom cries.

"That's the *Delta Queen*. It stops here a few times a year. Beautiful, isn't it? I never get tired of seeing that fine...looking boat," comments Aunt Noonie.

"It certainly is beautiful, and it's exceptionally beautiful today," smiles Mom. "I can see two black dogs on that boat. I'll just bet it's our Bear and Katie," she continues as she runs towards the magnificent boat pulling into the dock.

Bear and Katie are howling, jumping, and wagging their tails. They are so happy to be back where they started so many hours ago.

Bear heads straight for Aunt Noonie's table to see what she cooked for the party. Katie takes a dive in the river, jumps out and shakes herself off, then runs to join Bear, who has already begun to eat.

"Look at all of this food!" says Bear with a big lab smile. "We have fried chicken, Noonie's famous baked ham, chicken and dumplin's, corn bread, soup beans, hot rolls, pineapple upside down cake and blackberry cobbler. Ummm! ummm!"

Mom is happy to see Bear and Katie back at the reunion party and enjoying their meal, but she is worried about Dad and the kids. Will they find out that Bear and Katie got on another boat?

Noonie and the others assure her that everything will be fine.

Just as Bear and Katie finish eating, Dad's truck pulls up and everyone begins to climb

out. Bear can't believe her eyes.

"Look, Katie!" she yelps. "It's Gramps and Matthew!"

Bear and Katie run to Dad first. With their tails wagging in the wind, they jump and wiggle as they greet him. Dad hugs both of his happy labs.

Katie turns and runs to Matthew, jumps on him and knocks him to the ground, then sets to work, enthusiastically licking the boy on the face. Bear stops short of Gramps, then snuggles up close to her new friend.

"Well, well," says Dad. "I guess you and Matthew have made Bear and Katie very happy. I'm so glad you agreed to come along."

"Oh, by the way," says Gramps, "My name is Pierre Marcell II."

Bear and Katie stand stock-still. "Pierre Marcell II?" ruffs Bear.

"Pierre Marcell II?" echoes Katie. "That story you told us...Pierre Marcell, the great poker player who roamed the Ohio and Mississippi Rivers, was...your father?"

"That's right, Bear and Katie. He was my father, and he was Matthew's great grandfather."

"And Margrette was your mother?" cries Katie.

"That's right," answers Matthew. "That beautiful woman was my great grandmother."

"Who was Pierre Marcell?" asks Dad, mystified. "And who was this Margrette?"

"Pierre Marcell! You don't know who Pierre Marcell is?" laugh Bear and Katie.

Dad puts his arm across Gramps' shoulders.

"Well, maybe after you enjoy Aunt Noonie's country cookin' you can share the story of Pierre Marcell with the rest of us. I'm especially interested in hearing about Margrette," says Dad with a wink.

Bear and Katie look at Matthew and smile. They know that Matthew is proud of the stories his Gramps tells.

"Bear, I know we shouldn't have gotten on the boat earlier, but it was just so beautiful, I couldn't resist taking a look around," whines Katie, her head hanging.

"You're right about that, but I have to admit, we wouldn't have met Gramps and Matthew if you hadn't gone and gotten us in all that trouble," agrees Bear.

"We wouldn't have knocked all that food off the table. Although I must say the chicken was good," chuckles Katie.

"And we wouldn't have heard the story about Pierre Marcell," answers Bear.

"And we wouldn't have gone for that wonderful ride on the *Belle of Louisville*," ruffs Katie.

"Oh, don't forget the *Delta Queen*. <u>That</u> was awesome," grunts Bear.

"And there's nothing more fun than playing ball with Josh, Dirk, Jerry, Allison and Taylor," ruffs Katie.

"Don't forget Aunt Noonie's country cookin'," says Bear.

Everyone laughs, they enjoy listening to Bear and Katie talk about their afternoon's adventure..

"You know what, Bear? I really enjoyed myself today," ruffs Katie.

"I can't wait to come back again next year, and we haven't even left yet!" laughs Bear.

Bear and Katie amble over to a picnic table, turn a few weary circles and settle down. The two Black Labs are so tired they're practically asleep before they curl up beneath the table. Mom and Dad grin and shake their heads.

"We have our wonderful Bear and Katie back," says Dad. "Something tells me those two won't be going coon hunting with Uncle Tommy, Chief and Jane today. They're plumb tuckered out," he chuckles.

"Aren't they the greatest?" laughs Mom.

The End

About Our Riverboats

The Belle of Louisville
Legendary Lady

Built in 1914, the *Belle of Louisville* was originally called the *Idlewind*. She operated as a passenger ferry between Memphis, Tennessee, and West Memphis, Arkansas. During the 1920s, she traveled the Missouri River and then in 1934 the *Idlewind* returned to Louisville to operate a regular excursion schedule through

World War II. In 1947 the boat was sold and renamed the *Avalon*. For 13 years the *Avalon* pulled into ports all along the Missouri and Mississippi Rivers. In 1962 the *Avalon* was in horrible condition, but a Judge in Kentucky bought her at an auction for $34,000 and she was taken to Louisville to begin a new life. With it came a new name, *The Belle of Louisville*.

The Delta Queen

The *Delta Queen* is a National Historic Landmark, a veteran of World War II, and the only steamboat to travel through the Panama

Canal. She has hosted three Presidents and a Princess. The *Delta Queen* was built in 1927 and with 75 years on the river it was inducted into the National Maritime Hall of Fame in 2004. She remains in operation today, accommodating people during rides from New Orleans to Pittsburg.

The *Delta Queen* and the *Belle of Louisville* have been squaring off every year since 1963. Hundreds of spectators line both sides of the river on the Wednesday before the Kentucky Derby in Louisville, to watch these two magnificent boats power their way up the Ohio river for everyone to enjoy.

From the riverboat era

The *Arnold Hanners Collection*
Of the Boyd County Public Library

Bound for Huntington, the Delta Queen is seen here in old Lock 29, Ashland-Catlettsburg, in 1948. The photo was taken before the Greenup Dam was built, and Lock 29 has since been eliminated.

VIEW, STEAMER HOMER SMITH, LARGEST EXCURSION BOAT ON OHIO RIVER, MAYSVILLE, KY.

About Bear

Bear is gentle, caring, very intelligent and quick thinking. She always obeys the rules and loves playing the role of Katie's protector. Her hobbies include riding around with Dad, retrieving balls and chasing squirrels. Bear welcomes a pat on the head from everyone she meets. Bear, a female Black Lab/Shepherd mix, wandered her way to our doorstep when she was only six weeks old. Bear always wears a collar.

About Katie

Katie is fun loving, a bit too friendly, and is always getting into trouble. She loves her best friend Bear and knows Bear will always come to her rescue. Katie finds trouble everywhere she goes. Her hobbies are swimming, retrieving balls and frisbee. She was rescued at the last minute from a dog pound when she was six months old. Katie is a female Black Lab. Katie prefers to wear a scarf.

About the Author

Loni R. Burchette was born in Ashland, Kentucky. It was only when she moved to New Hampshire that she finally  found a place she could love as much as the beautiful "Blue Grass State" she hails from. Along with her husband and four of her five children, she now makes the Lakes Region of New Hampshire her home. Her hobbies are writing, art and traveling.

About the Illustrator

Patricia Sweet-MacDonald was born in Clearwater, Florida. She moved to New Hampshire in 2002, with her husband,  Michael and two children, Alison and Brendan. She started painting at age 5 and has never quit.

Future Bear and Katie Books

A Day at the Beach and Katie Gets Arrested

Bear and Katie at the Kentucky Derby "Run for the Roses"

Lost in the White Mountains

Bear and Katie See the Big Apple

In the Badlands with Mr. Wanbli (Eagle)

A Day with Mato the Bear

Visit our website at www.bearandkatie.com

Other books by
Loni Burchett

Bear and Katie in The Great Searsport Caper
Bear and Katie in A Day at Nestlenook Farm
Bear and Katie in A Day With Friends
Released 2004